Uncle's Bakery

Written by Dana Meachen Rau

Illustrated by Janie Baskin

Reading Advisers:

Gail Saunders-Smith, Ph.D.

Dr. Linda D. Labbo, Department of Reading Education,
College of Education, The University of Georgia

LEVEL B

A COMPA

EARLY

D1174364

For Nathan, Travis, Abigail, and Bradley

A Note to Parents

As you share this book with your child, you are showing your new reader what reading looks like and sounds like. You can read to your child anywhere—in a special area in your home, at the library, on the bus, or in the car. Your child will associate reading with the pleasure of being with you.

This book will introduce your young reader to many of the basic concepts, skills, and vocabulary necessary for successful reading. Talk through the details in each picture before you read. Then read the book to your child. As you read, point to each word, stopping to talk about what the words mean and the pictures show. Your child will begin to link the sounds of the letters with the look of the words that you and he or she read.

After your child is familiar with the story, let him or her read the story alone. Be careful to let the young reader make mistakes and correct them on his or her own. Be sure to praise the young reader's abilities. And, above all, have fun.

Gail Saunders-Smith, Ph.D.
Reading Specialist

Compass Point Books
3722 West 50th Street, #115
Minneapolis, MN 55410

Visit Compass Point Books on the Internet at *www.compasspointbooks.com* or e-mail your request to *custserv@compasspointbooks.com*

Library of Congress Cataloging-in-Publication Data
Rau, Dana Meachen, 1971–
    Uncle's bakery / written by Dana Meachen Rau ; illustrated by Janie Baskin.
        p. cm. — (Compass Point early reader)
    Summary: A young girl visits her uncle's bakery with her mother and together they use all their senses to enjoy their visit.
        ISBN 0-7565-0119-9 (hardcover : library binding)
        [1. Bakers and bakeries—Fiction. 2. Senses and sensations—Fiction.] I. Baskin, Janie, ill. II. Title. III. Series.
    PZ7.R193975 Un 2001
    [E]—dc21   2001001595

Let's go in Uncle's bakery.

He loves to bake with me!

I'll use all my senses: hear, smell, touch, taste, and see.

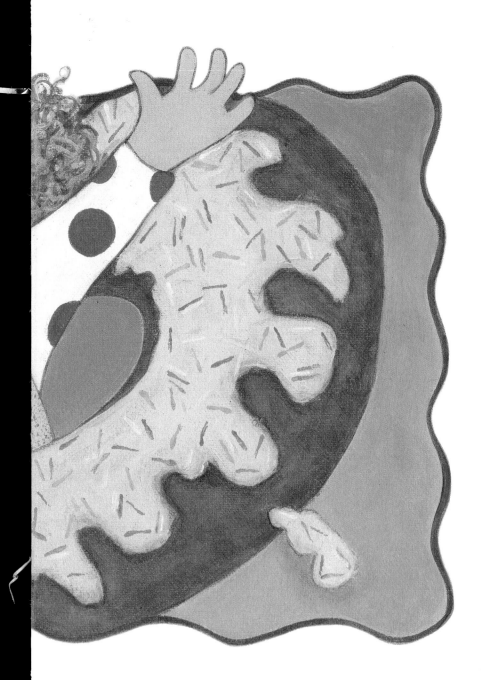

Hear the pans.

Hear the whisk
bang against the bowl.

See the berries.

See the nuts
pour into the dough.

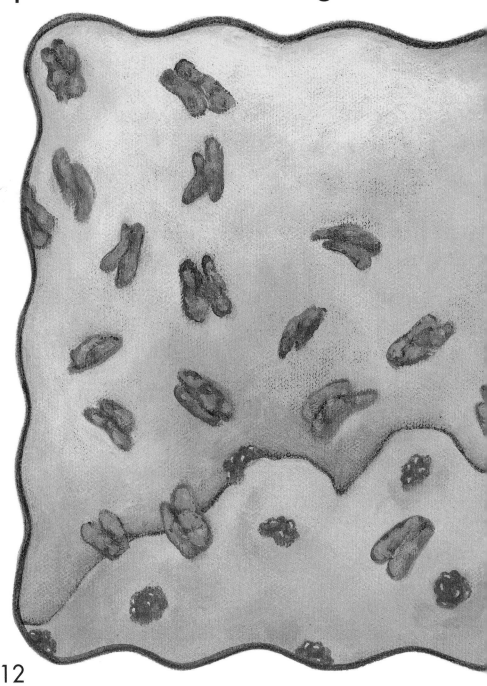

13

Smell the kitchen.

Smell the buns bake
until they're brown.

Touch the bag.

Touch the icing and drizzle all around.

Taste the buns.

Taste the icing dripping down the sides.

I love Uncle's bakery.

Next let's make some pies!

More Fun with Baking

Baking is a wonderful activity you can share with your child. It introduces early math concepts through measuring, the art of creation, and the importance of cleaning up when you are done!

On the next page is a recipe for a tasty pie that you and your child can make together.

Share your pie with each other and talk about how you used all of your senses. What did the pie **look** like before you baked it? What about after? What was your favorite **smell**—the nutmeg? The apples? The cinnamon? Did you **hear** the spoon mixing in the bowl or the crinkling sound of foil? Does syrup **feel** sticky? Does flour feel soft? Does your pie **taste** yummy?

Tasty Apple Pie

Refrigerated pie crust
6 cups of apples, any kind
1 tablespoon flour
½ cup sugar
¼ cup maple syrup
2 teaspoons cinnamon
¼ teaspoon nutmeg

Heat the oven to 400°. Help your child peel, core, and cut the apples into small slices. Dump them into a large bowl. Then put all of the other ingredients (except the pie crust!) into the bowl and mix everything all together.

Unfold and lay one pie crust into a pie plate. Pour the apple mixture into the crust. Then, lay the other pie crust over the top. Tuck the edges in, and push them down with a fork all around the pie. Bake the pie in the oven for 20 minutes. Then cover the edges of the crust with foil. Bake it for 25 minutes more until it is brown.

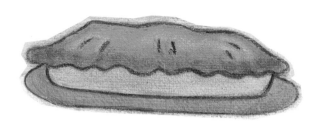

Word List

(In this book: 51 words)

against
all
and
around
bag
bake
bakery
bang
berries
bowl
brown
buns
dough
down
dripping
drizzle
go

he
hear
I
I'll
icing
in
into
kitchen
let's
love
loves
make
me
my
next
nuts
pans

pies
pour
see
senses
sides
smell
some
taste
the
they're
to
touch
Uncle's
until
use
whisk
with

About the Author
Dana Meachen Rau enjoys baking. Recently she made snickerdoodle cookies and used all of her senses. She loved the feeling of the sticky dough. She loved the smell of the cookies in the oven. She loved the sound of the buzzer when they were ready. She loved tasting them when they cooled. And she loved the sight of her clean kitchen when she was all done. After she was done baking, she brought some cookies into her home office in Farmington, Connecticut, and wrote on her computer.

About the Illustrator
Janie Baskin loves to bake. She had so many desserts in her house she had to buy an extra freezer to store them. One day she started selling her cakes and cookies. Although it was a lot of work, it was also a lot of fun. The only thing Ms. Baskin likes creating more than good things to eat is artwork. Sometimes she paints pictures of food. Sometimes she uses food to make dyes for her pictures. Ms. Baskin lives with her daughter and husband in Northbrook, Illinois. She takes yummy treats to her friends when she goes to visit.